For Tara Walker, the most kindred of spirits.
I knew when we first talked about this book that it was for you. — S.O'L.

For my giant girl, Béatrice — M.L.

Tundra Books, an imprint of Penguin Random House Canada Young Readers,
a division of Penguin Random House of Canada Limited

Library and Archives Canada Cataloguing in Publication

Title: Gemma and the giant girl / Sara O'Leary ; [illustrated by] Marie Lafrance.
Names: O'Leary, Sara, author. | Lafrance, Marie, illustrator.
Identifiers: Canadiana (print) 20200310410 | Canadiana (ebook) 20200310445
ISBN 9780735263673 (hardcover) | ISBN 9780735263680 (EPUB)
Classification: LCC PS8579.L293 G46 2021 | DDC jC813/.54—dc23

Published simultaneously in the United States of America by Tundra Books of Northern New York,
an imprint of Penguin Random House Canada Young Readers,
a division of Penguin Random House of Canada Limited

Library of Congress Control Number: 2020945227

Edited by Tara Walker with assistance from Margot Blankier
Designed by John Martz
The artwork in this book was drawn in graphite pencil and colored in Photoshop.
The text was set in Ashbury.

Printed in China

www.penguinrandomhouse.ca

1 2 3 4 5   25 24 23 22 21

Penguin
Random House
tundra | TUNDRA BOOKS

Gemma
AND THE
Giant Girl

WORDS BY
Sara O'Leary

PICTURES BY
Marie Lafrance

tundra

Gemma lived in a very nice little house
and had a very nice little life.

She had always slept in the same room,
had always played with the same toys
and had always worn the same clothes.

Things had been the same forever and ever.

"Will I grow up one day?" Gemma asked her parents.
"You will always be our little girl," they said.

Momma and Poppa told her stories about
a time when there had been giants.

They said that outside their house was
another larger house.

Gemma tried to imagine it, but it made
no sense.

There was nothing outside her window.

And then one day…

Gemma felt the house move.
She saw everything slide . . .
first in one direction . . .
and then the other.

There was something outside the house.
"A giant!" said Momma and Poppa.

Gemma didn't believe in giants.
But she really wanted to see one.

And then there she was. A giant girl.
   The stories were true!
   "I wonder if *she* is somebody's little girl?"
whispered Gemma.

After that, life changed. New things appeared in the house all the time.

Some were too big. Some were too small. Some were just right.

Some of the new things were nice.

Some were less nice.

The family all got
new clothes.

And then new,
new clothes.
Gemma felt like
a whole new girl.

Once, a book appeared. It was so big that it took both her parents to turn the pages, but it was full of wonderful pictures.

"Those are trees," said Momma.

"Those are stars," said Poppa.

"That's the moon," they murmured together.

Gemma thought that life really couldn't get any more interesting.
But then one night, it did.

Suddenly Gemma was outside looking
in at her own little house.

She could see Momma and Poppa
frozen with fear.

She could see her room and her bed
and her little lamp.

Gemma was in a room that was quite a bit like her own room, only much, much larger.

And then she was gently set down.

"Look!" said the giant girl. "The world!"

The world was bigger than Gemma could ever
have imagined.
"Trees," she thought. "Stars. The moon!"

Gemma couldn't believe how beautiful it all was.
And yet...
"Home," she said. "I want to go home."

And the next thing Gemma knew she was back in her own little bed, in her own little room, in her own little house.

She was very happy to be home again with Momma and Poppa.

She liked her little house. She liked her little life.

And that night Gemma dreamt that
outside her window was the world.